This book belongs to

Diedre & Louis

Presented by

Aunt Debbie

Date

May 11, 2014 Mother's Day

To my Snuggle Bugs, who are my greatest treasure,
my Little Buddies, who smiled for the camera,
a Mom who says I can,
and the adventurer in all of us

Visit us at shadowmountain.com

Library of Congress Cataloging-in-Publication Data

Cooley, Judy.
  Mom Says I Can / Judy Cooley.
     p. cm.
  Summary: A young boy imagines himself in many brave and intrepid roles
as he searches for the world's greatest treasure, before finding it
right at home.
  ISBN 978-1-59038-872-3 (hardcover : alk. paper)
  [1. Mothers and sons—Fiction. 2. Adventure and adventurers—Fiction.
3. Imagination—Fiction.] I. Title.

PZ7.C7766Mo 2008
[E]—dc22   2007041160

Printed in the United States of America
Inland Graphics, Menomonee Falls, WI

10 9 8 7 6 5 4 3 2

Mom Says I Can

Mom Says I Can

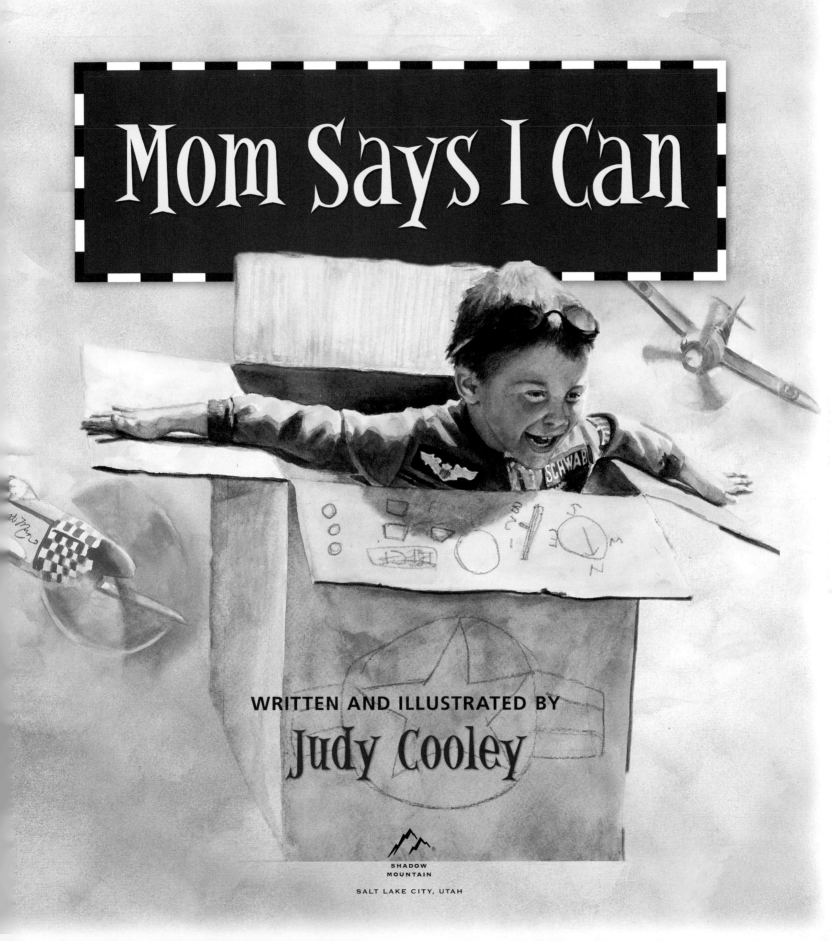

WRITTEN AND ILLUSTRATED BY

Judy Cooley

SHADOW
MOUNTAIN

SALT LAKE CITY, UTAH

Hi, I'm Max

Mom calls me Snuggle Bug,

And Dad calls me Little Buddy.

But today I'm Super Cool Max,

Best Treasure Hunter Ever!

I'm going to find

The World's Greatest Treasure.

Mom says I can!

I'm a Pirate

I sail a pirate ship

And say things like "Aarghh,"

Just like a real pirate.

I have the secret map to find

The World's Greatest Treasure.

Mom says I'm so tough!

I'm a Cowboy

I ride a horse

And wear cowboy boots and a hat.

I yell, "Giddy-up, Lightning!"

Just like a real cowboy.

I'm going to find

The World's Greatest Treasure.

Mom says I'm the fastest ever!

I'm a Pilot

I fly airplanes way up high in the air.

I can do loop-de-loops,

Just like a real pilot.

I will fly all over the world and find

The World's Greatest Treasure.

Mom says I'm so amazing!

I'm the King of the Jungle

Look at me swing—

I'm not afraid of anything!

Just like the real king of the jungle.

I'm going to search the deepest jungles and find

The World's Greatest Treasure.

Mom says be careful!

I'm a Knight in Shining Armor

I have a big sword and a shield

To fight dragons,

Just like a real knight.

I'm going to find

The World's Greatest Treasure.

Mom says I'm her hero!

I'm a Superhero

This is NOT my underwear!

See my cape and mask?

I can run super fast, fly really high,

And I'm the strongest man ever,

Just like a real superhero.

With my special powers I'll find

The World's Greatest Treasure.

Mom says I can't go out in my underwear!

I'm an Indian Chief

I sleep in a teepee

And shoot a bow and arrow.

I can do anything,

Just like a real Indian chief.

I will hunt and find

The World's Greatest Treasure.

Mom says I'm so brave!

I'm a Spaceman

Can't you tell by my

Supercharged rocket pack and

My supersonic blasting laser gun?

Just like a real spaceman.

I'll blast off to find

The World's Greatest Treasure.

Mom says I'm cool!

Who do we have here?

Mom asks.

No costumes or maps?

No horses or planes or rocket packs?

No grand adventure today?

Aren't you Super Cool Max, Best Treasure Hunter Ever?

I tell her no,

I want to be your Snuggle Bug.

I have a blankie and a book.

Mom, will you hug me?

Mom says she loves me!

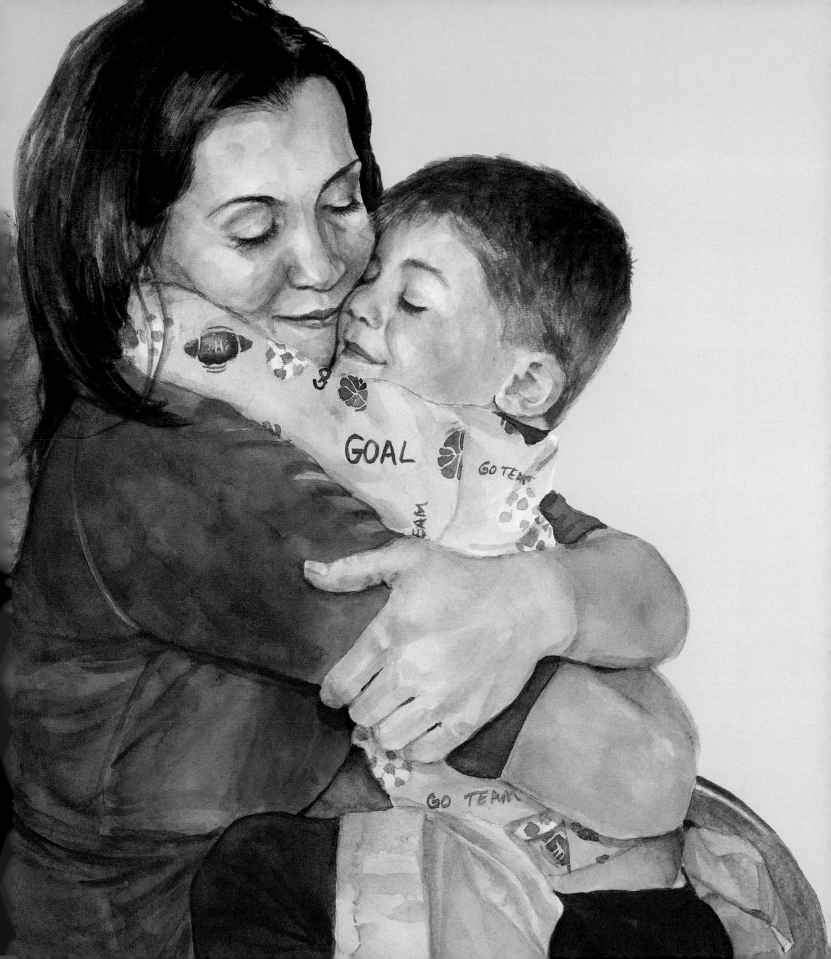

That's it, Mom. I found it!

The World's Greatest Treasure!

Do you know where it is?

It was right here all the time—

It's you, Mom!

Can I be your Snuggle Bug forever?

Mom says I can!